Danny D was proud and very happy! "Look, Papa Stu, I have an A and a gold star on my paper."

Papa Stu was happy too. He smiled.
He patted Danny D's head.
Then Papa Stu stooped down so
he could see right into Danny D's
eyes. Papa Stu said,
"That's great, Danny D.
I'm proud of you.
You really know that lesson.
Did you know that God
knows that lesson too?
In fact, God ALWAYS
gets a star on his paper!"

Danny D could hardly
understand that.

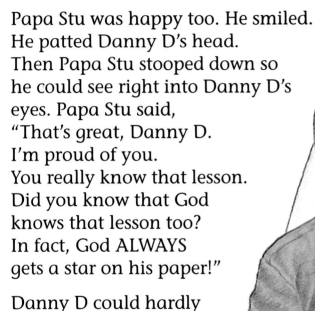

Papa Stu and Danny D
went to the candy store.
Danny D didn't know which candy
to choose.
There were so many kinds.

Papa Stu smiled.
He patted Danny D's head.
Then Papa Stu stooped down
so he could see
right into Danny D's eyes.
"Danny D, did you know
that God knows
how much candy there is
in the whole world?
In fact, God knows
EVERYTHING!"

Danny D
and his lunch
ride the
bus to school.
Every day
Mommy packs
a yummy lunch
for Danny D.
One day
Danny D forgot
his lunch.
It was an
AWFUL
FEELING!

Papa Stu said,
"I'm sorry you had such
a bad day, Danny D.
Did you know that God
never forgets his lunch?
In fact, God
always remembers
EVERYTHING!"

Danny D wished he could
remember everything
and never again
forget his lunch.

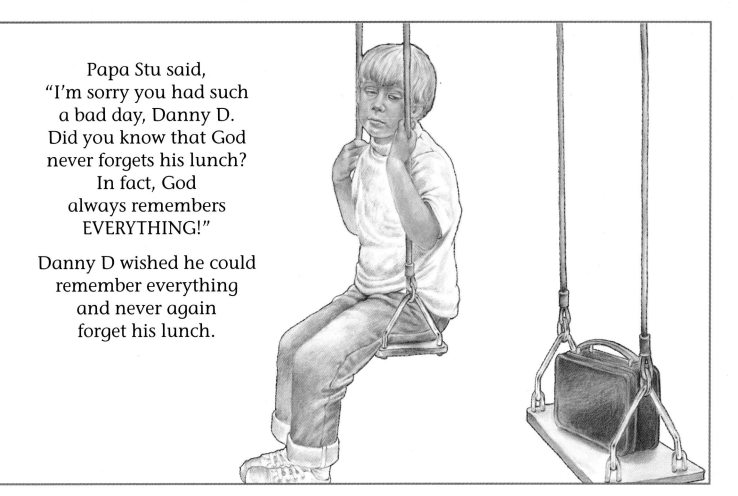

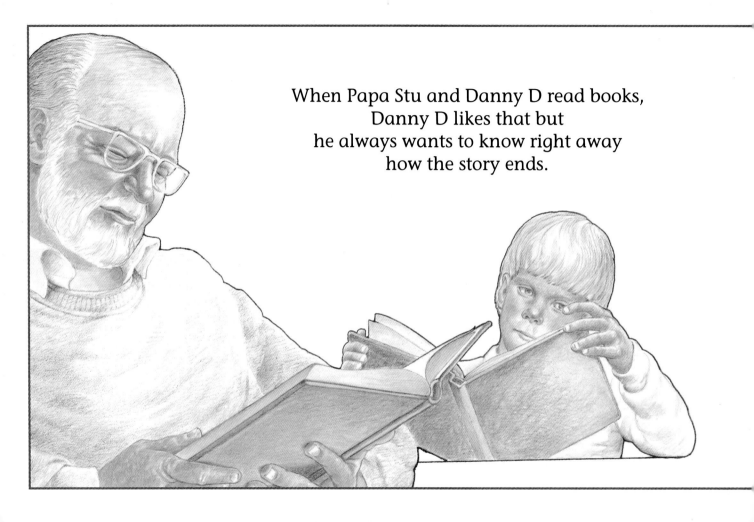

When Papa Stu and Danny D read books,
Danny D likes that but
he always wants to know right away
how the story ends.

Today Papa Stu smiled. He patted Danny D's head.
Then Papa Stu stooped down so he could see right into Danny D's eyes.
Papa Stu said, "Danny D, did you know that God knows the end of all
the stories in the world without reading them?
In fact, God knows EVERYTHING!"

Danny D said, "I think
God is VERY clever!"

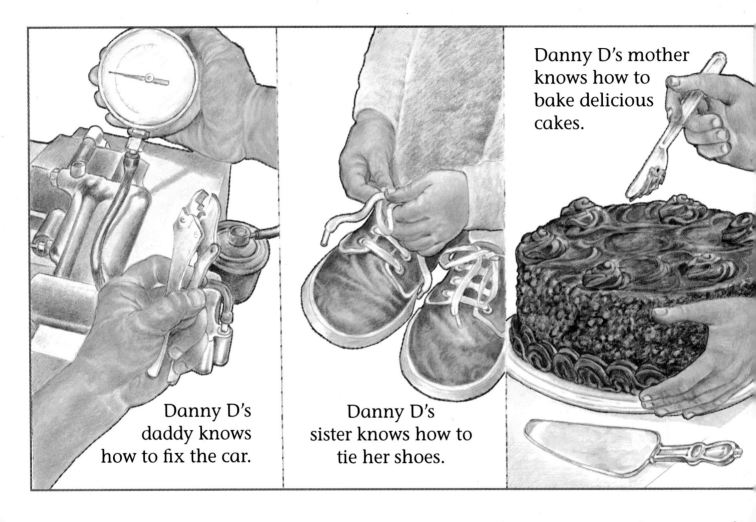

Danny D's daddy knows how to fix the car.

Danny D's sister knows how to tie her shoes.

Danny D's mother knows how to bake delicious cakes.